FOR THE MISFITS
AND THE NITWITS
FOR THE ODD
AND THE STRANGE
FOR THE HOPEFUL
AND THE HOPELESS
STAY FLAWED
NEVER CHANGE ♡

TABLE OF CONTENTS

The Nightmare Nursery	4
Nine Rejected Inventions	12
Itchy	26
The Wall	28
The Tomorrow Mirror	36
Finnigan Fullerbutton	60
Failed Act	68
The Floating Castle	70
Eyeball Soup	76
Backwards High	78
Marty the Mime	88
Bird-Headed Freak	96
The Do Not Pet Shop	98
The Switch	120
My Cozy Coffin	126
Everything Store	128
The Monster Under My Bed	138

The Nightmare Nursery

There exists a garden where all dreams are grown
Where everyone's deepest desires are shown

But amidst the flowers of love, fame, and flying
Resides a dark forest, grim and terrifying

It's called the Nightmare Nursery
Where fears are never-ending
A garden of magic and mystery
Where our greatest horrors get tending

The plants may look normal upon first glance
Until you see that they have teeth and hands

They whisper to you in a voice so sweet
And lure you in so you can't retreat

They breach your mind to take root and grow
Into full-blown nightmares all dreamers know

But the wise few who tend to the land
Are not afraid of the terrors at hand

For the nursery is a place of growth
That helps them face their fears the most

If you're ever in that garden of dreams
Don't be afraid of the nightmares and screams
Don't cover your eyes, don't cover your ears
Embrace them and you will conquer your fears.

Nine Rejected Inventions

We now have **Nine Inventions**
Which were forever rejected
Dazzling innovations
That were never perfected

Number One is a flamethrower
That cost a hefty price
But instead of shooting flames
It only shoots ice

Number Two is a painting
Of a flower you can smell
But take one sniff
And you'll cower and you'll yell
For soon, vines will grow
Out your ears and your nose
And leaves will replace
All your fingers and your toes

This key made from bones
Takes spot **Number Three**
But I would not touch
This skeleton key
It used to belong
To a famed explorer
The only thing it unlocks
Is your deepest horror

Step into this jacuzzi
To experience **Number Four**
It has jets on every side,
And even on the floor
But don't get too close
They're a bit out of sorts
I know this is gross,
But they'll suck in your shorts

Number Five on that mat
Was once a top seller
It's a very old hat
With a built-in propeller
With a push of a button
You surely will fly
But coming back down
Is where things go awry

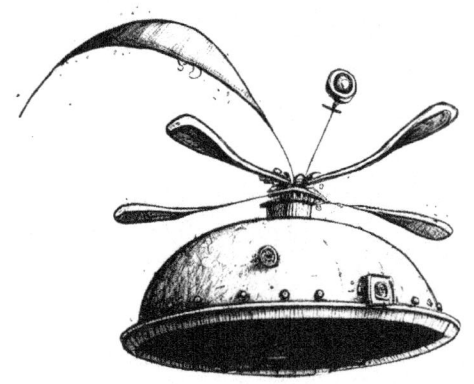

Number Six is over there
That way on the right
A light switch that can turn
Each day into night
But once it is flicked,
It can never switch back
Where once there was light,
Will be forever pitch black

This twisted oak tree
Was once a portal to heaven
But as you can see
It's now invention **Number Seven**
For when you crawl through
The giant hole in its trunk
You immediately get sprayed
By a nasty little skunk

Holding a cane
Is a favorite, **Number Eight**
A talkative crane
That can tell you your fate
But this type of crane
Only tells when you'll die
Which is quite a pain
Because it's known to lie

We're at the end of the line
And I'm sure you may wonder
Didn't I say there were nine,
Where's the last number?

Well just step in this cage
To witness our newest addition
You may want to sit
Or find a comfortable position
Because there's no way out
And nowhere to go
And people are en route
To enjoy the show

I'm sorry to say,
I forgot to mention
That you yourself
Are the 9th Rejected Invention.

ITCHY

I awoke this morning with a tinge of regret
And the most annoyingly itchy itch on my neck

I itched with my nails, then a fork, then a rake
But nothing would work, except a sharp wooden stake
At last I achieved a moment of relief,
But this itch relief was oh so brief

The icky rash began to swell and burn
And now I wished for the itch to return

I ran to grab a cup of cold water
But once it splashed it just made it hotter
I had doused my neck to ease the pain
But now it became a huge red stain

Every itch, every scratch, oh what a curse
Like a mosquito bite, but ten times worse

If only I had known how itchy it would be
When I let that pretty vampire feed on me.

I live in a town surrounded by a wall
Made of cement and brick, one hundred feet tall

They say it's to keep us safe, that it's for our own good
That we must fear what awaits beyond our neighborhood

And based on the many intimidating sounds
The most haunting rumors have been whispered around

Some say it's a monster
Some say it's a ghost
Others say it's a demon
Who will cook you like toast

But I refuse to suffer this fear of the unknown
This myth that holds us back from leaving our comfort zone

I needed to know what lies ahead
Is it something of beauty or something to dread?

The wall was tall and smooth and cold
No cracks, no gaps, no grips to hold

So I chopped some trees and built a tall ladder
I was really quite pleased, I couldn't be gladder

I reached and I climbed and thought of the other side
Long hills of tulips where magic insects reside

A land where dragonflies would dance in the sun
While spiders made art with the webs they had spun

Trees would sing songs to the birds who sang back
And flowers would glow when the night's sky turns black

The waterfalls fall backwards so you could swim right up
And rivers taste like sherbet that you could drink with a cup

As I reached the top
My town felt so small
A sea of houses and shops
Held back by a wall

How will they come
To prosper and grow
Dreading the things
They do not know

I slid down the back
My feet touched the ground
And from the pitch black…
Came a guttural sound

They tried to warn me
That the grass isn't always greener
And sure enough, the eyes staring back
Looked much much meaner.

THE TOMORROW MIRROR

Today was the most special day of them all
For the circus was in town at the pier past the mall

Quinn saved up for months to buy his own ticket
And awoke before dawn so he wouldn't miss it

He thought of the flying trapeze over the shark-infested pool
And the firestick jugglers balancing on a one-legged stool

And the infant who could lift 50 times her weight
With the elephant who could dance and roller skate

But when he arrived at the colorful grounds
He was surprised to discover, there were no crowds

There was, however, a line of thousands around the block
Curving and twisting all the way down the dock

Quinn approached a lion tamer wearing a mask
And tapped the man's foot, shouting up to ask,

"How come the ferris wheel over there isn't packed?
Why is there no attendance at the death-defying acts?"

The tamer twirled his mustache and pointed with his cane
Up past the elephants and the lions he had trained

He took off his mask and bent down to explain
These patrons have no interest in being entertained

"They're all in line for today's main attraction
Some unbelievable sight, with a guaranteed reaction"

Sure enough, there it was, a tiny blue tent at the end of the pier
With a beaming neon sign that read "The Tomorrow Mirror"

A magical mirror that shows what your future holds
Displaying how events yet to come will soon unfold

"But why care about tomorrow
When there's so much to see today?"
The tamer pleaded while pointing
To the sign for 'Lion Ballet'

But Quinn got in line and patiently waited
Eager to see how his life was fated

As the sun set and the moon shone bright
The line ahead had no end in sight

He imagined his future and how it would look
"Would I become president, would I write a book?

Would I be rich, I wonder who I'd marry,
Would it be Suzy or Kara, I hope it's not Sherry"

"Maybe I'll live in a tree with a really high view
In a house made of branches held together by glue

Or perhaps I'll build a boat so light it could fly
And sail it up above every cloud in the sky

Or maybe I'll stay here closer to the ground
And explore new lands that have yet to be found"

At last, Quinn's turn had finally arrived
His chance to learn what his future prescribed

He stared at the piece of long wavy glass
Expecting he'd be at the top of his class

But he saw no awards, no fame, not a plaque
The only thing he saw was himself staring back

Quinn turned to the magician near the entrance flap
And shouted toward him and the rabbit in his hat

"This silly broken mirror is no magic at all
No glimpse of the future, no magic eight ball"

"Ah but that is indeed the very next day
For midnight is now just one minute away"

So Quinn looked at himself from one minute ahead
Wishing he'd listened to what the tamer had said

And now the circus was being packed away
Not a tent nor a clown remained on display

He had spent his whole day so focused on the next
The exhibits he came for, he never even checked

The tamer marched over
A heart full of sorrow
"See, kid, you lost a day
Worrying about tomorrow

If you weren't so concerned with the future,"
He said standing tall,
"You would have realized that today
Was the most special day of them all."

FINNIGAN FULLERBUTTON

Finnigan Fullerbutton,
Who lived in the upside down house on Rightside Up Way,
Was a curious person who went outside only once per day

He'd stare at the sky for an hour or two
What he was looking at, no one knew

When the neighbors would interrupt
To ask why his house wasn't right-side up

Finnigan would simply say with a frown:
"Perhaps it is WE who are upside down"

Strange noises emerged from his house every day
But what he was doing, he'd never say

And one night while the town slept
Finnigan would act on the secret he kept

They all awoke to a loud rumbling sound
And Finnigan's house was nowhere to be found

No one knew why his house disappeared all of the sudden
No one except… for Finnigan Fullerbutton.

FAILED ACT

A magician had once
Sawed this lady in half
The big crowd erupted,
They shouted and laughed
But for her, the big act
Wasn't nearly as fun
For the magician never
Put her back together
As one.

THE FLOATING CASTLE

Once upon a time
In a castle above the sea
Lived Princess Adeline
At the top of tower three

But on the night she turned sixteen
Adeline returned home quite late
Which greatly upset the Queen
Who gathered the kingdom to celebrate

The Queen sent Adeline away to her tower
Who marched up the steps with defiant power
She didn't care about parties or taking the throne
She simply wished to be left alone

She slammed her door so hard
It caused the castle to shake
Even those in the yard
Could feel the Earth quake
Overnight, a single crack grew
Then more and more
Until there were more than a few

The tower broke from the cliff
And fell into the sea
Floating adrift
She was finally free

She looked through the hole
Where the door once lay
To see the castle becoming
Farther and farther away

Adeline thought "This is great!"
"No more parents to rule my fate"

Day became night
Night became day
Not a soul within sight
As she floated away

Alone at last
It was quite nice
But her wish come true
Had come at a price

As time went on
And waves crashed strong
The most beautiful views
Became the loneliest cruise

She glanced up at the sky
To a shooting star
It looked to be close
Yet somehow so far
And this time instead
Of wishing to be alone
She simply wished
To go back home.

Eyeball Soup

Whenever you next dine in a group
Might I recommend the eyeball soup?

Amongst its garlic and leaves of basil
Are eyes that are brown, green, blue and hazel

A tinge of sour, a dose of sweet
The eyes all glower whilst you eat

Following your movements as you chew
Floating around in their steamy stew

Really forcing you to stop and think
About what goes into your food and drink

To consider where it's sourced and how it is made
Into a savory course fancily displayed

And next time no matter what you are consuming
You will ponder these hard questions that are looming

For it's impossible not to gain a new point of view
When you have looked at your dinner looking right back at you.

BACKWARDS HIGH

Welcome to Backwards High
Where nothing is what you'd expect
Where getting 100 on your test
Means getting zero correct

But first there are some things to know
Before you do attend
Some basic rules to follow
And tips I'd recommend

Here, the popular kids are losers
And it's cool to have no friends
We write with pencils on computers
And the weekend never ends

The boys all ask the girls
To the Sadie Hawkins dance
And pop quizzes get announced
Several weeks in advance

We all call Principal Dunn
By his first name Jeff
And our cafeteria is run
By a famous 3-star chef

Exams are wacky adventures
Instead of reading comprehension
And only faculty members
Get punished with detention

There's no such thing as homework
Or need for hallway passes
And did I mention students
Are the teachers of our classes?

You may think that we are strange
And our school's unorthodox
But here at Backwards High
We think outside the box

And if you're just like me
And you think backwards too
Then Backwards High might be
The perfect school for you

But we regret to inform you
Your application's been rejected
So welcome to Backwards High
Where that means you've been accepted!

MARTY THE MIME

Once upon a time
In a town with no crime
Lived a boy named Marty
Known as Marty the mime

Marty hadn't always been this way
But as he walked home alone one day

He took a disastrous wrong turn
That prompted immediate concern

For he stepped outside the town borders
Straight into the witches quarters

Just as he tried to let out a scream
His eyes were met by a bright purple beam

A callous spell cast out from a wand
In the hand of the witch standing next to the pond

Marty ran as fast as he could
Belting forward into the woods

He returned to town, where he tried to speak
But nothing came out, not even a squeak

Days passed, then months, then years
He'd yell into their ears, but still no one could hear

Without any semblance of a voice
Marty was left with only one choice

To turn his curse into his vocation
One without need for verbal narration

And so he settled on Marty the mime
And that's how he's been known for quite some time.

Bird-Headed Freak

Let me introduce
The bird-headed freak
She looks like a girl
But her nose is a beak
Don't stare for too long
She's sensitive no doubt
So just run along
Or she'll peck your eyes out.

The Do Not Pet Shop

All I want is a pet
From the pet shop in town
The old store with the step
And the door that is round

I do not know what kind
That I'd want to have yet
But I'll know when I see it
I'll know what to get

I entered the shop
Right through the round door
And saw a cute pet
Chase its tail on the floor
I reached out to pet
But heard someone shout "Stop!"
Pointing up at the sign:
"The Do Not Pet Shop"

"That pet over there
Might look like a dog"
Said the shopkeeper man,
Who was holding a frog

"But in fact it is not,
It is really part snake
You can tell by its tail
And the rattle it makes

We have pets of all kinds
But not ones to pet
It's the one rule we have
So please don't forget

There's a horse with a mane
Made of really sharp spikes

And a fish that's see-through
And rather ghost-like

This Crabtapus here
Deserves your applause
It has eight tentacles
With ends that are claws"

"Those sound pretty great
But they don't catch my eye
I was thinking I'd wait
For one that can fly"

"If you want one with wings
You should just say the word
Have you seen any thing
Like a flame breathing bird?

Or maybe you'd prefer
One demanding less practice
Like a spiky green cat
Whose fur is like cactus"

"Perhaps there are pets
Less painful to hold?"

"How about this frost mouse?"

"Ouch! Its skin is ice cold!"

"I'll say it again,
Just one final time,"
The shopkeeper said
Pointing back to the sign

"We have pets of all kinds
But not ones to pet
It's the one rule we have
So please don't forget"

With so much to see
I surveyed the store
And from a red crate
I heard a loud roar

"What's in there?" I then asked
The elderly keeper
"The most dangerous pet,
That's where I do keep her"

"Will you open it up,
Just one little crack?"
"I suppose if you keep
Your hands at your back"

So I clasped both my hands
As he opened the crate
And I saw not two eyes
But instead I saw eight

She had fur that was fuzzy
Like a soft little sheep
And I knew then and there
That this pet I must keep

Then a bell made a sound
From the round entry door
And the man turned around
To the front of his store

So this was my chance
And the last chance I'd get
To reach out and touch
With just one little pet

So fluffy,
    so comfy,
        so silky,
            so fuzzy,
                So–

CHOMP

The shopkeeper heard
Turning quickly around
Only to find
I was not to be found

"There's one rule we have
That you mustn't forget"

"I know, I know…
You have pets of all kinds
But not ones to pet."

THE SWITCH

So you're probably wondering why
There are giant sea creatures in the sky

It's been like this in my town
Since our world flipped upside down

One day the sea became the sky
And to this day no one knows why

Legend has it, there's only one fix
Beneath the ground is a switch that exists

And now my town's last hope of staying alive
Is if one of us steps up and takes the dive

But everyone fears what awaits beneath...
The most sinister creatures - with the most sinister teeth.

MY COZY COFFIN

I'd jump in every night
Snuggled down with a smile
I loved the way it felt
To be wrapped up in style

To be hugged on both sides
It's better than a bed
And the greatest part is
You don't have to be dead

I know you think it's weird
I lay in here often
But nothing's cozier
Than my cozy coffin.

EVERYTHING STORE

There's something here for everyone
No matter what their kind
Whatever your quirk, our items will work
Let's see what we can find

We have roller coasters for leprechauns
And breath mints for a dragon
And if you're in need of zombie salons
You better bet we have 'em

We have mirrors for vampires
And toilet paper for mummies
Want to try on our mermaid pants
Or taste our tasteless gummies?

We have ski masks with one eyehole
They're perfect for a Cyclops
And just in case its eye gets dry
We also carry eye drops

We have sneakers for clowns
That weigh forty-four pounds
And sandals fit for a troll
We have dinosaur boots
And high heels for your moose
In case you care for a stroll

We have shampoo designed for werewolf hair
And a ceiling fan for demons
We also have UFOs over there
Should you wish to see them

So peruse all you'd like
Buy some shoes or a bike
Just leave your items at the door
Cuz at the end of the day
I'm sorry to say
That nothing can leave our store

For we may offer hornets nests,
An invisible dress,
And a Bigfoot pedicure
But the only item
We do not possess
Is a working register.

THE MONSTER UNDER MY BED

There's a monster under my bed
Who is really quite horrific
I can't get him out of my head
So let me be more specific

He's rather big and hairy
With three eyes that glow in the dark
His teeth are very scary
Just like those of a great white shark

But as I've grown older,
His methods have changed
His tactics turned bolder,
And rather deranged

Instead of belting out
Some big thunderous roar
He lets out a whisper
While lying on my floor

"Hey, are you up?"
My Monster will ask
Lifting my bed
So I can't relax

"Ugh please, Monster,
I'm trying to go to sleep"

"Just one question,
I won't make another peep"

"Okay fine what is it?"
I asked from above

"Do you think that you will
Ever find true love?"

This is what he always does
He tries to make me worry
As my uncomfortable thoughts
All rush in in a flurry

He reminds me of all the things
I still need to do
Citing embarrassing moments
Right out of the blue

The places I've never been
And promises I've broken
All the games I never win
And my thoughts left unspoken

Memories I've left behind
And the people I've upset
All the times I wasn't kind
And the moments I regret

"Monster, can you PLEASE
Just let me go to bed?
Why must you put these
Scary thoughts in my head?"

"But what about everything
You still have to do?
Let's worry about the death
Of all those you ever knew"

"Can't you ever talk
About something nice?
Or put me at ease
With words of advice?"

"I wouldn't be a monster
If it's all peaches and cream
You should really be thankful
I no longer make you scream"

"Please let me sleep,
I have had a rough day
I can't count sheep
Unless you go away"

Just as I begin to snore,
My Monster groans again,
"I'm sorry about before,
Can I still be your friend?

I know you feel you don't fit in
I know you get in your own way
And that is how it's always been
And it gets harder every day

But there's something I'd like to share
And then off to sleep you go
Out of all the kids I scare
You're the coolest kid I know"

"Thanks, Monster," I said
For the first time ever
"We can still be friends."

"Really?! Friends Forever?!"

For now this was enough
To calm all my sorrows
All my other worries
Could wait til tomorrow

As my eyes finally closed
And my mind dozed off
The Monster under my bed
Woke me with a cough

"Hey remember that one time
You tried talking to your crush
But froze and stared and peed your—
"MONSTER FOR THE LAST TIME SHUSH!"